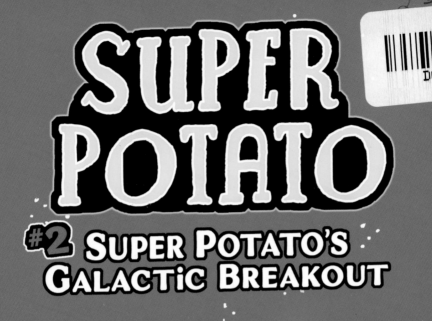

SUPER POTATO

#2 SUPER POTATO'S GALACTIC BREAKOUT

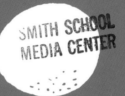

ARTUR LAPERLA

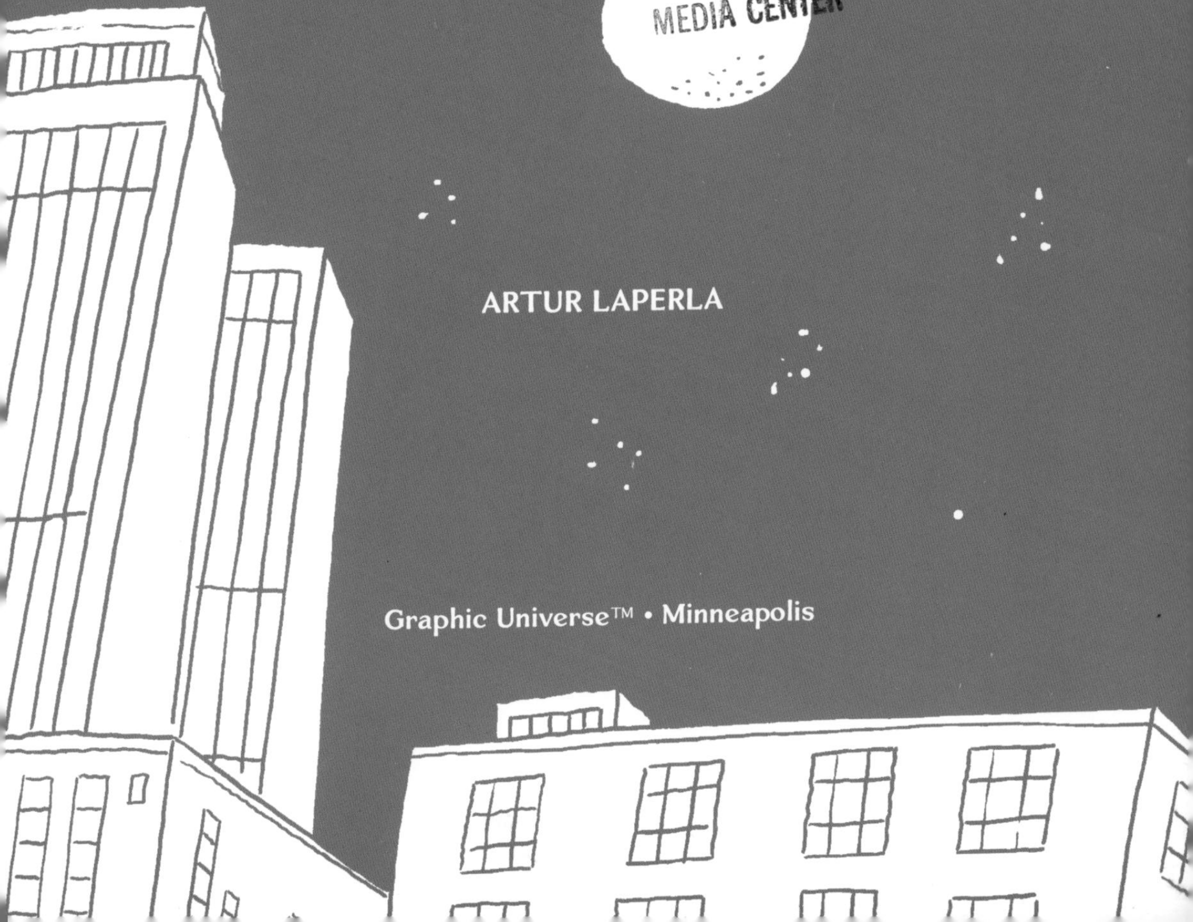

Graphic Universe™ • Minneapolis

Story and illustrations by Artur Laperla
Translation coordinated by Graphic Universe™

First American edition published in 2019 by Graphic Universe™

Copyright © 2012 by Artur Laperla and Bang. Ediciones. Published by arrangement with Garbuix Agency.

Graphic Universe™ is a trademark of Lerner Publishing Group, Inc.

Graphic Universe™
A division of Lerner Publishing Group, Inc.
241 First Avenue North
Minneapolis, MN 55401 USA

For reading levels and more information, look up this title at www.lernerbooks.com.

Main body text set in CCWildWords 8.5/10. Typeface provided by Comicraft.

Library of Congress Cataloging-in-Publication Data

Names: Laperla (Artist) author, illustrator.
Title: Super Potato's galactic breakout / Artur Laperla.
Description: First American edition. | Minneapolis : Graphic Universe, 2018. | Series: Super Potato ; #2 | Summary: "After an evil alien abducts Super Potato, the hero must escape from a collection of rare outer-space animals" —Provided by publisher
Identifiers: LCCN 2017043535 (print) | LCCN 2017055590 (ebook) | ISBN 9781541523807 (eb pdf) | ISBN 9781512440225 (lb : alk. paper) | ISBN 9781541526464 (pb : alk. paper)
Subjects: LCSH: Graphic novels. | CYAC: Superheroes—Fiction. | Human-alien encounters—Fiction. | Potatoes—Fiction. | Humorous stories. | Graphic novels.
Classification: LCC PZ7.7.L367 (ebook) | LCC PZ7.7.L367 Su 2018 (print) | DDC [Fic]—dc23

LC record available at https://lccn.loc.gov/2017043535

Manufactured in the United States of America
1-42291-26141-6/22/2018

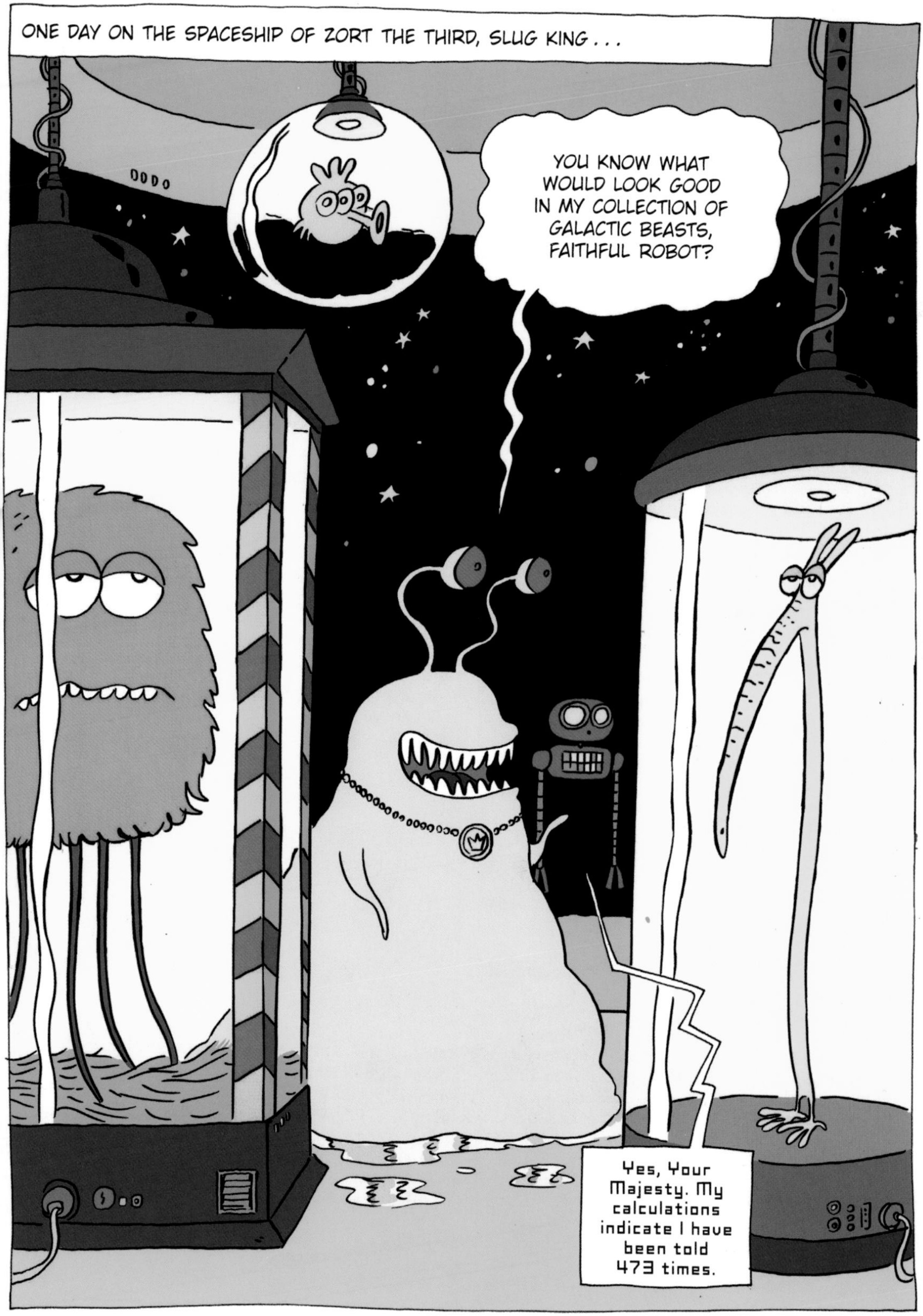
ONE DAY ON THE SPACESHIP OF ZORT THE THIRD, SLUG KING . . .
YOU KNOW WHAT WOULD LOOK GOOD IN MY COLLECTION OF GALACTIC BEASTS, FAITHFUL ROBOT?
Yes, Your Majesty. My calculations indicate I have been told 473 times.

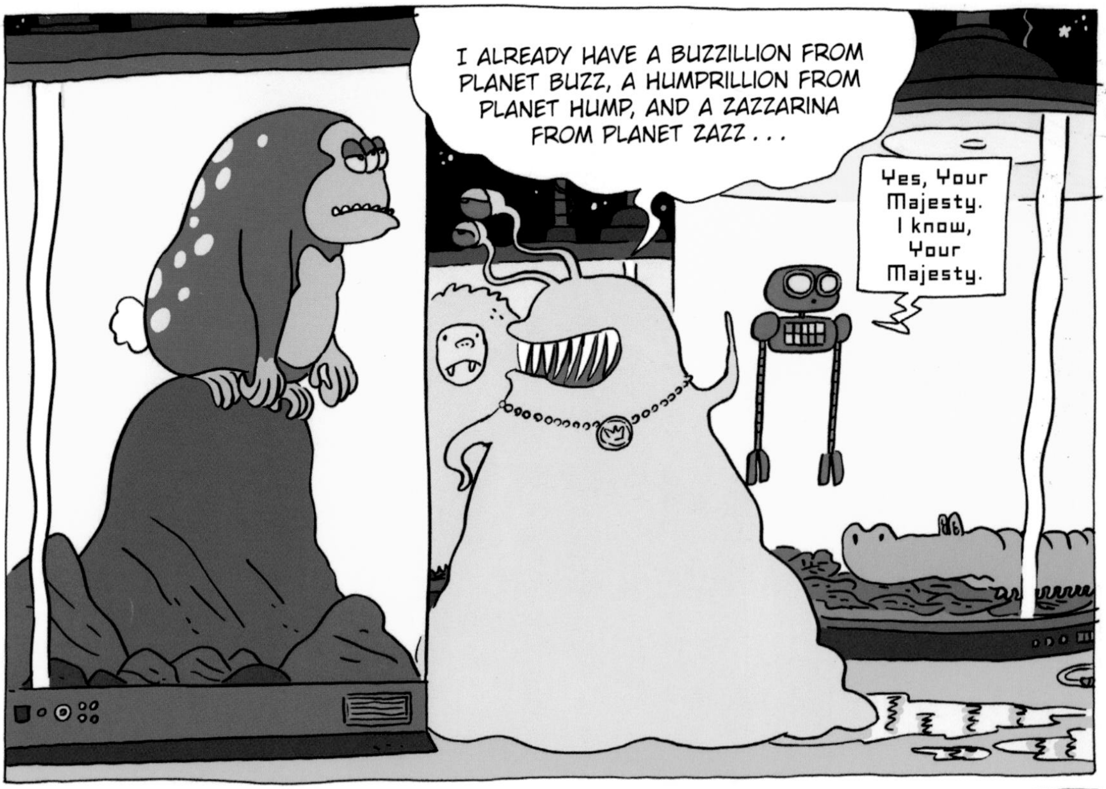
I ALREADY HAVE A BUZZILLION FROM PLANET BUZZ, A HUMPRILLION FROM PLANET HUMP, AND A ZAZZARINA FROM PLANET ZAZZ . . .
Yes, Your Majesty. I know, Your Majesty.

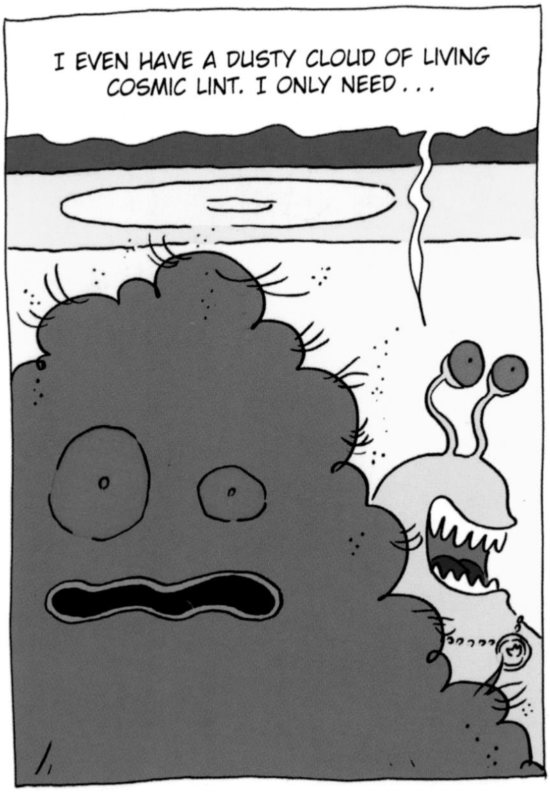
I EVEN HAVE A DUSTY CLOUD OF LIVING COSMIC LINT. I ONLY NEED . . .

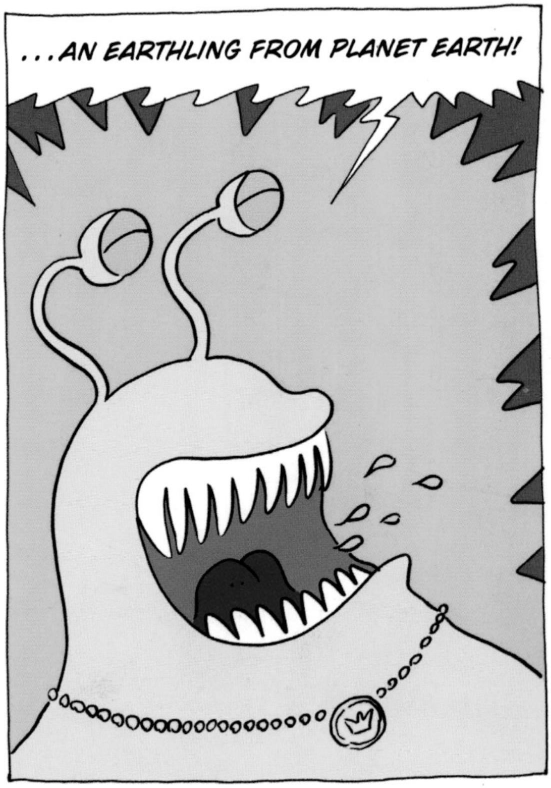
. . . AN EARTHLING FROM PLANET EARTH!

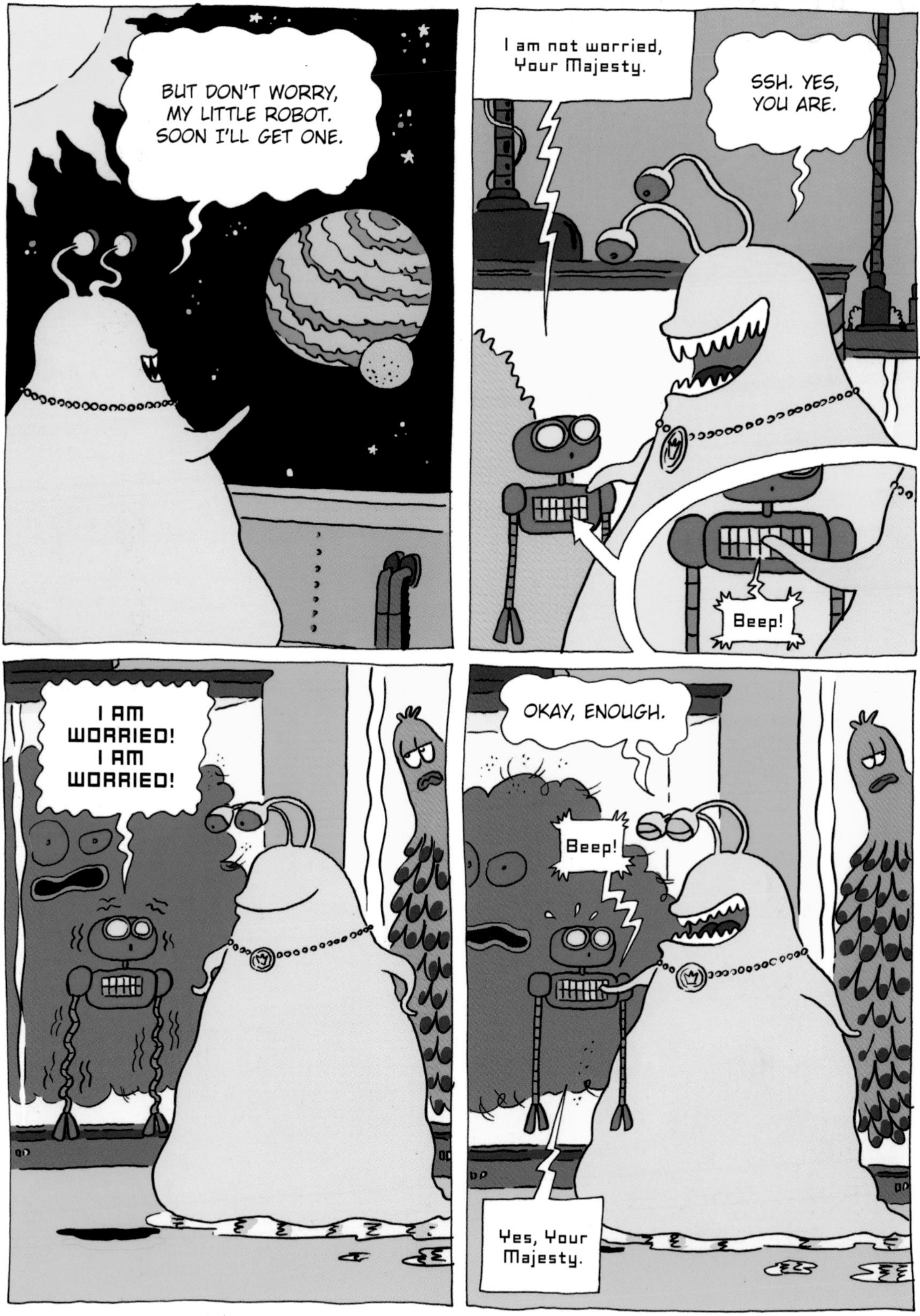
BUT DON'T WORRY, MY LITTLE ROBOT. SOON I'LL GET ONE.
I am not worried, Your Majesty.
SSH. YES, YOU ARE.
Beep!
I AM WORRIED! I AM WORRIED!
OKAY, ENOUGH.
Beep!
Yes, Your Majesty.

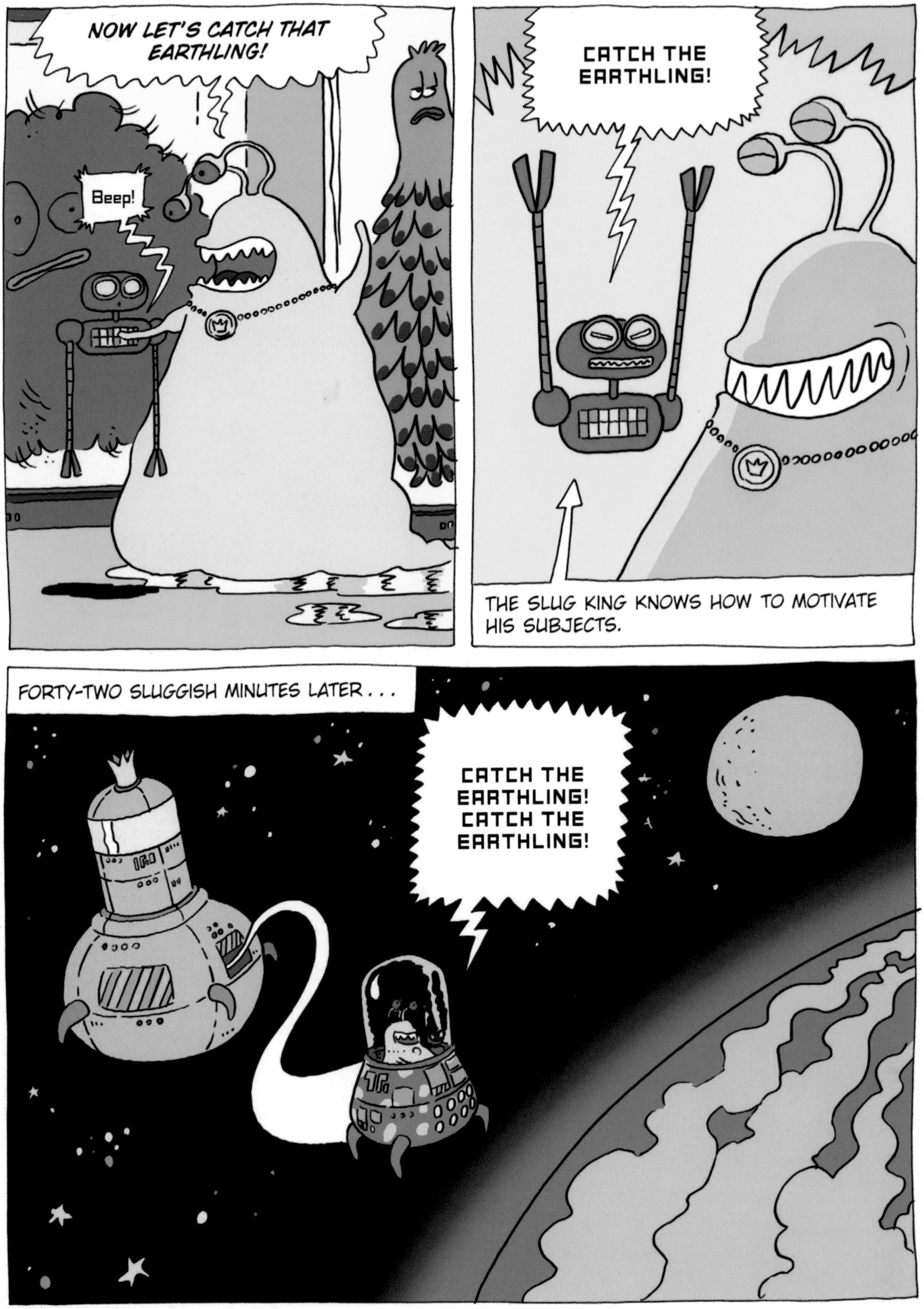
NOW LET'S CATCH THAT EARTHLING!
Beep!
CATCH THE EARTHLING!
THE SLUG KING KNOWS HOW TO MOTIVATE HIS SUBJECTS.
FORTY-TWO SLUGGISH MINUTES LATER . . .
CATCH THE EARTHLING! CATCH THE EARTHLING!

MEANWHILE, AT SUPER POTATO'S PLACE, OUR HERO IS DOING A BIT OF WEIGHT LIFTING . . .

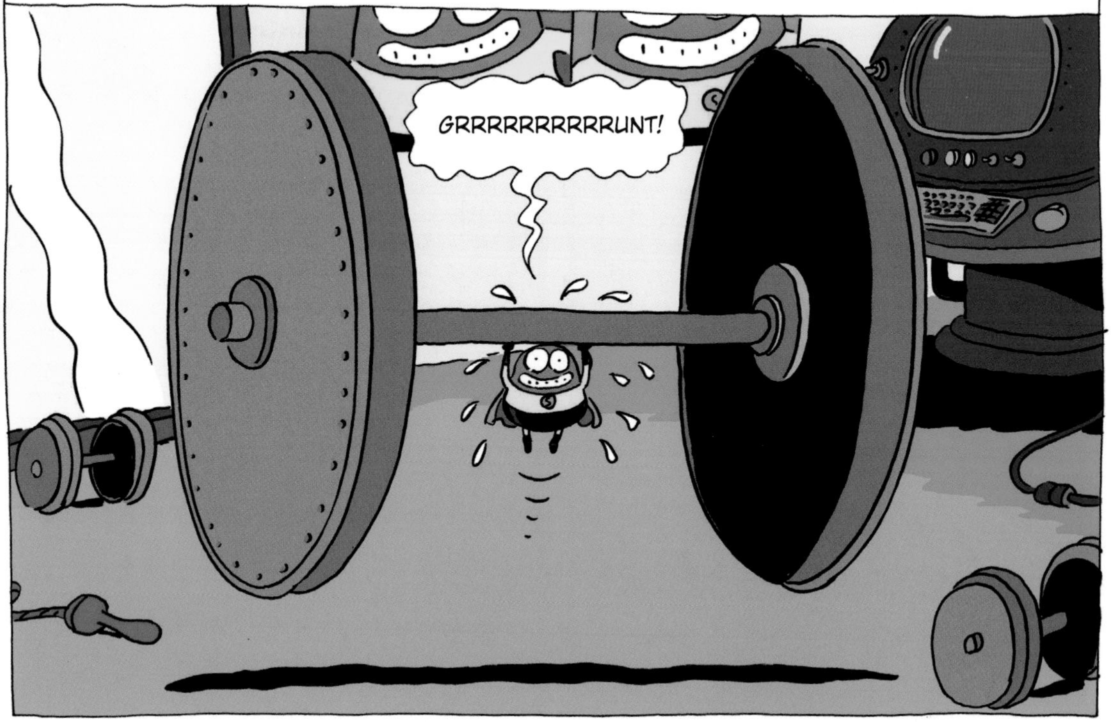
GRRRRRRRRRRUNT!

. . . DOING SOME PUSH-UPS . . .

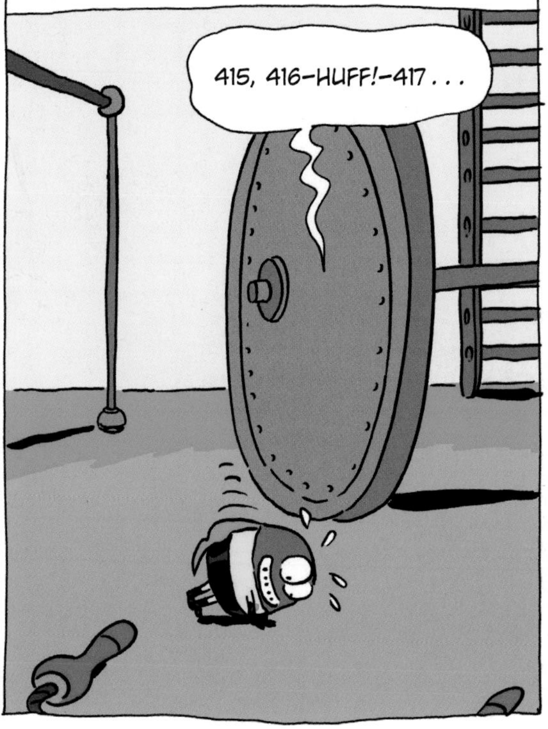
415, 416–HUFF!–417 . . .

. . . AND FLYING A FEW MILES TO STAY IN SHAPE.

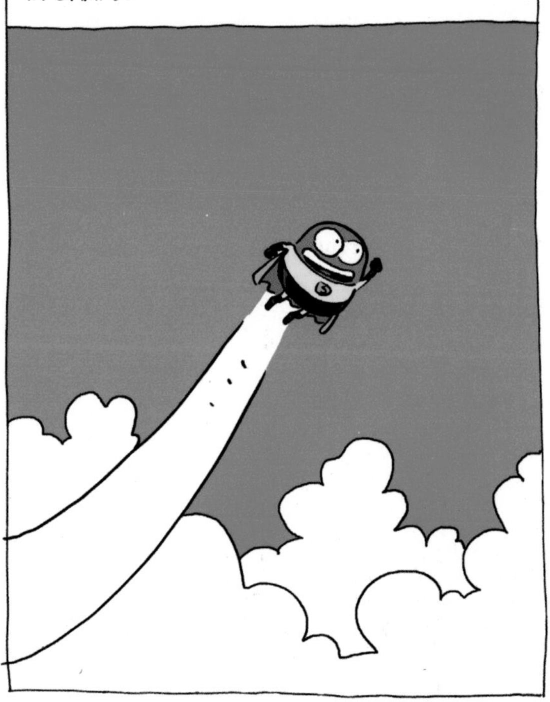

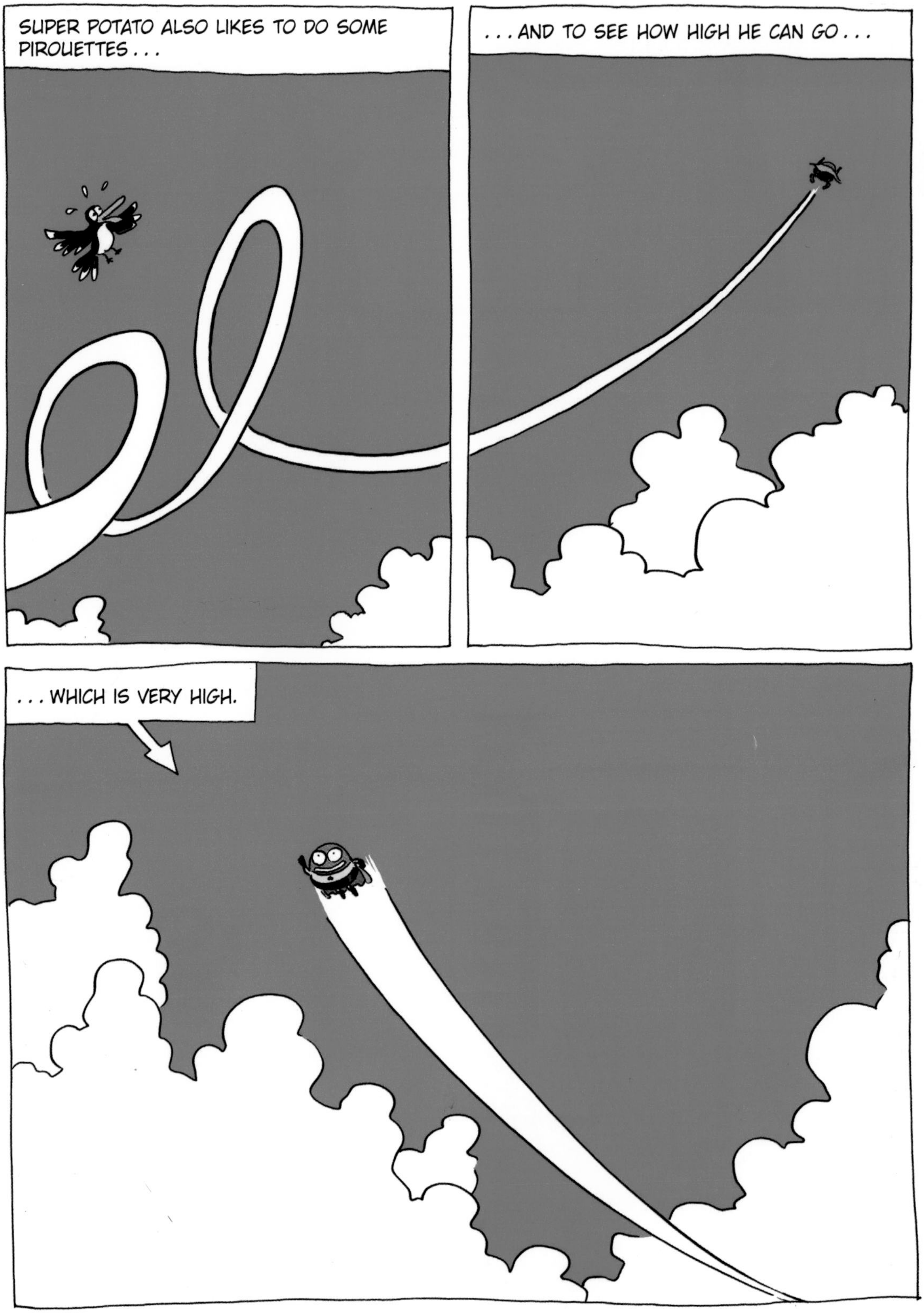
SUPER POTATO ALSO LIKES TO DO SOME PIROUETTES . . .
. . . AND TO SEE HOW HIGH HE CAN GO . . .
. . . WHICH IS VERY HIGH.

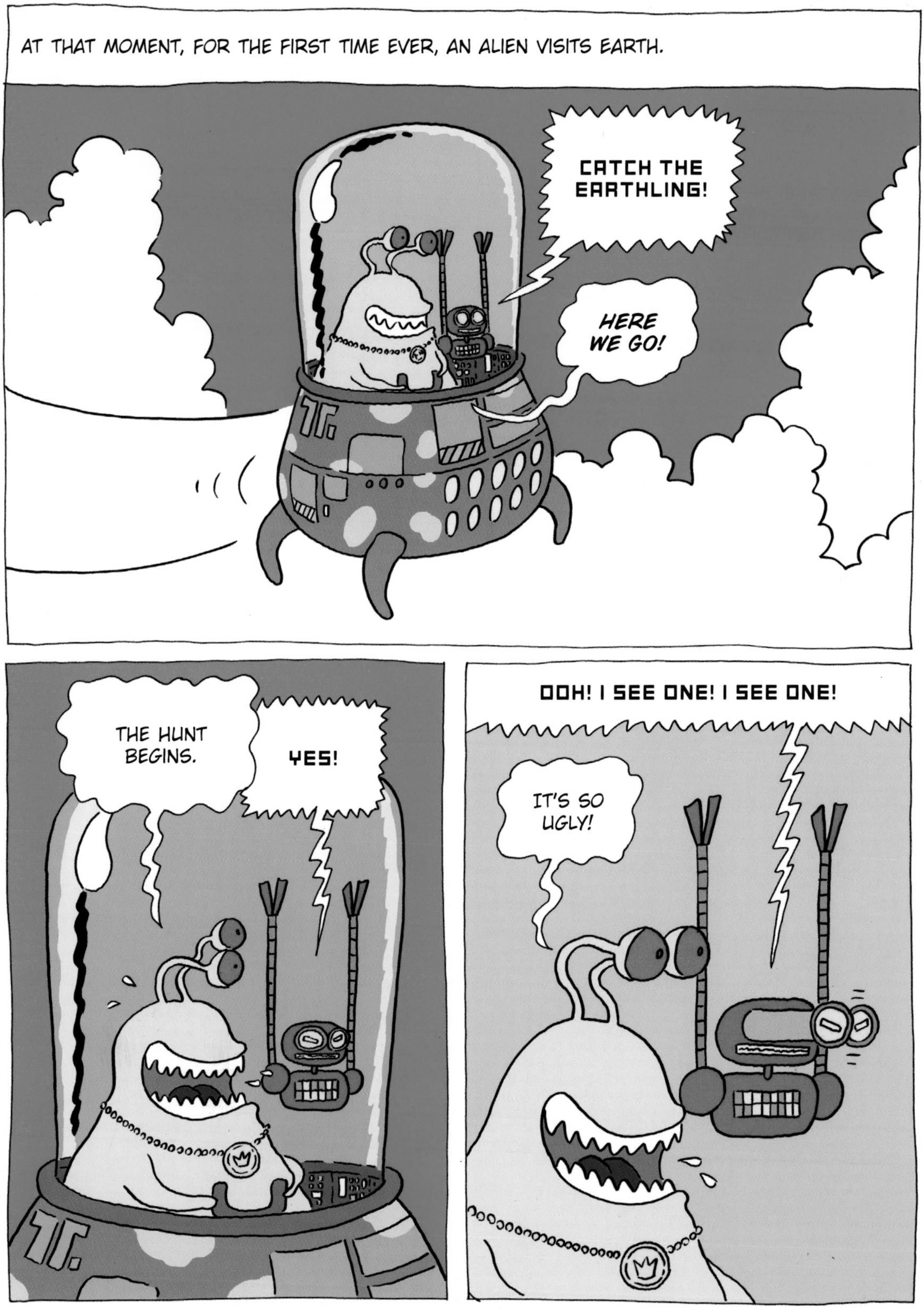
AT THAT MOMENT, FOR THE FIRST TIME EVER, AN ALIEN VISITS EARTH.
CATCH THE EARTHLING!
HERE WE GO!
THE HUNT BEGINS.
YES!
OOH! I SEE ONE! I SEE ONE!
IT'S SO UGLY!

12

14

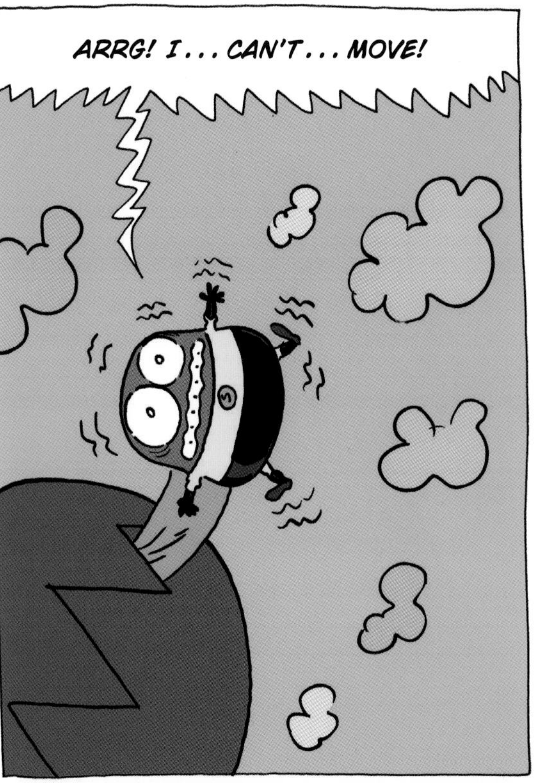
ARRG! I . . . CAN'T . . . MOVE!

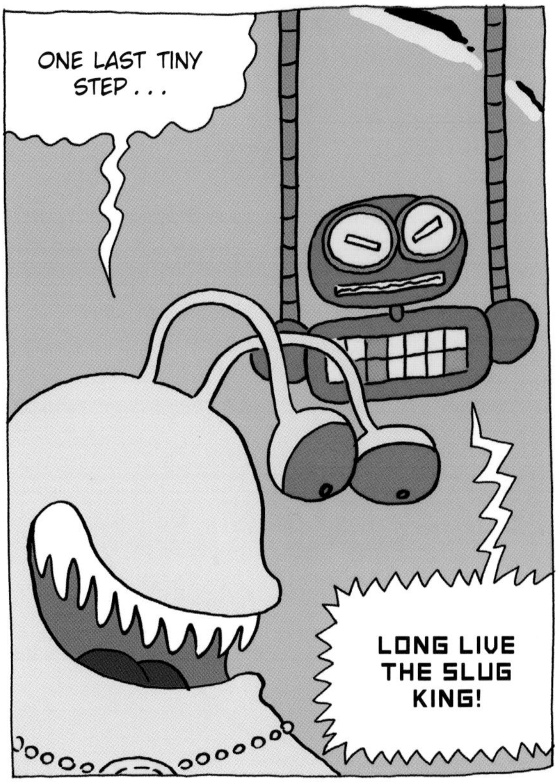
ONE LAST TINY STEP . . .
LONG LIVE THE SLUG KING!

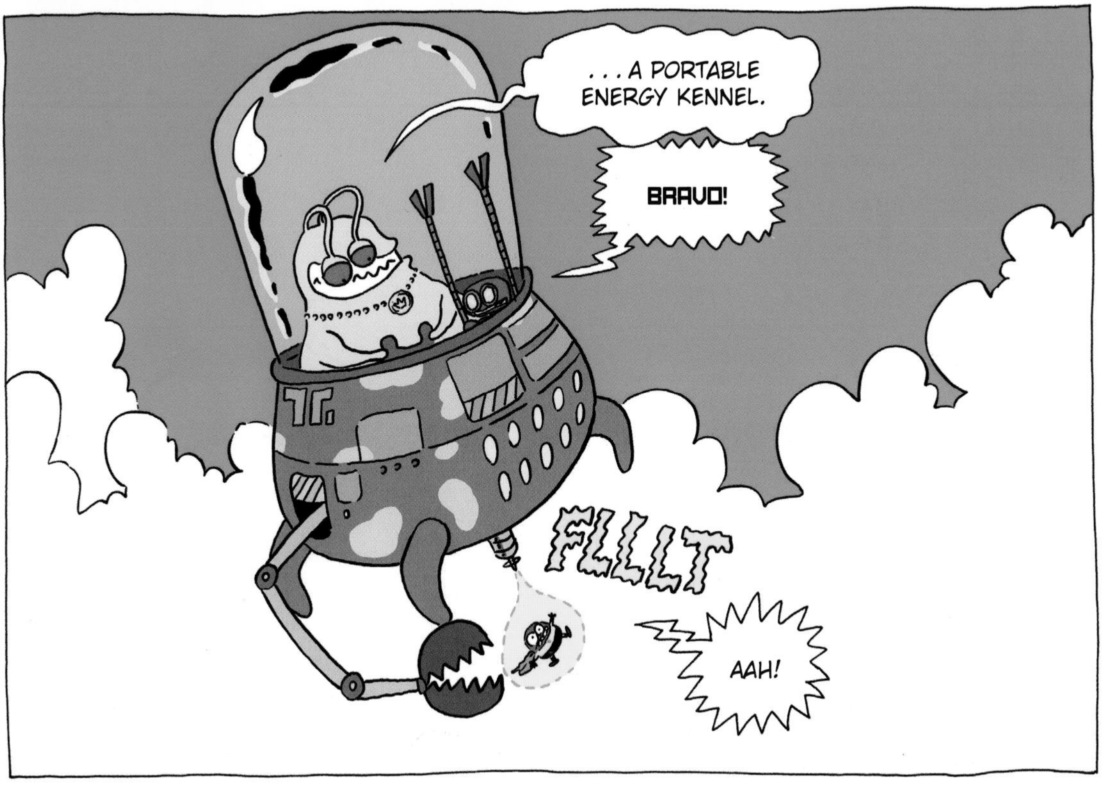
. . . A PORTABLE ENERGY KENNEL.
BRAVO!
FLLLT
AAH!

17

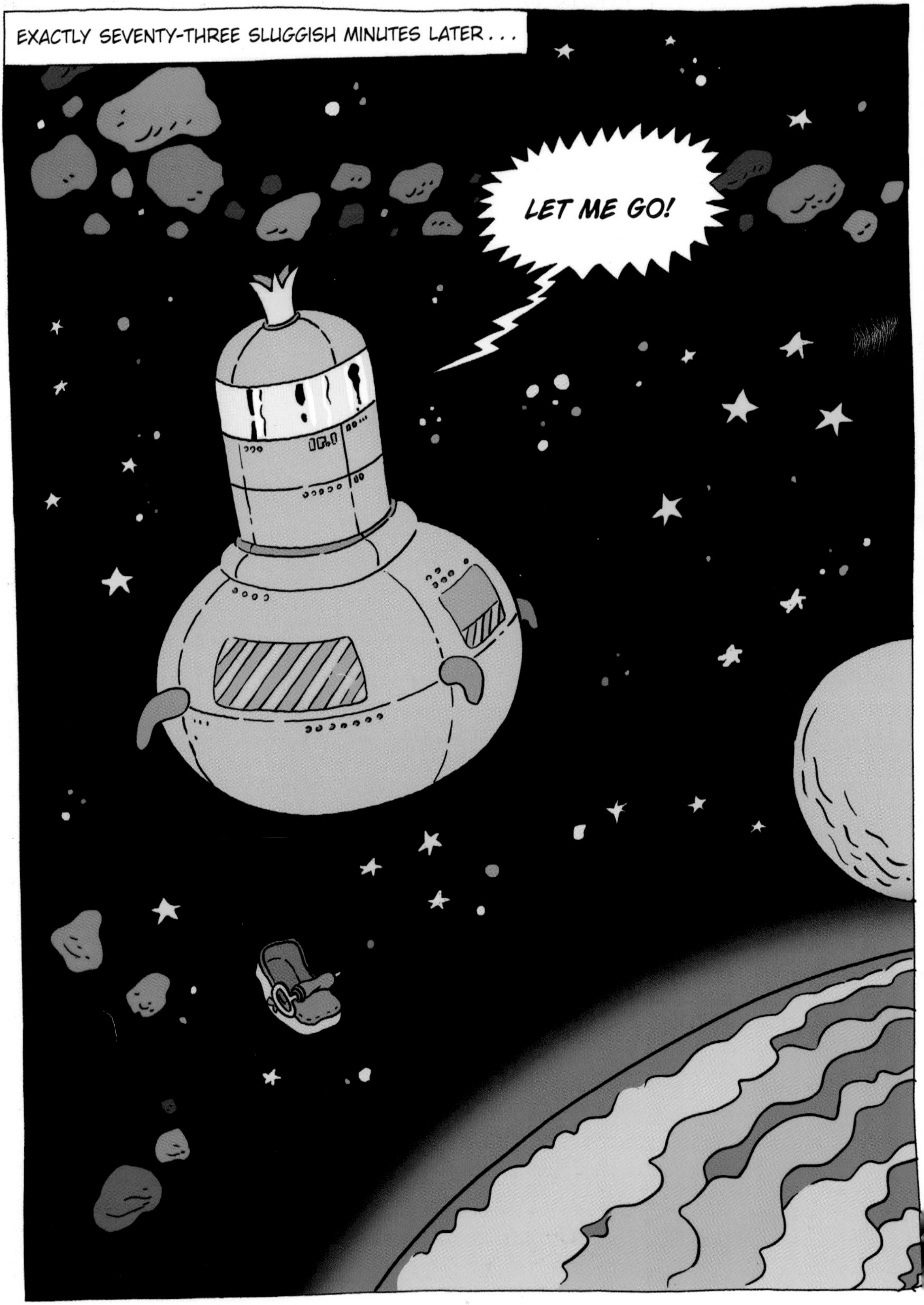
EXACTLY SEVENTY-THREE SLUGGISH MINUTES LATER . . .
LET ME GO!

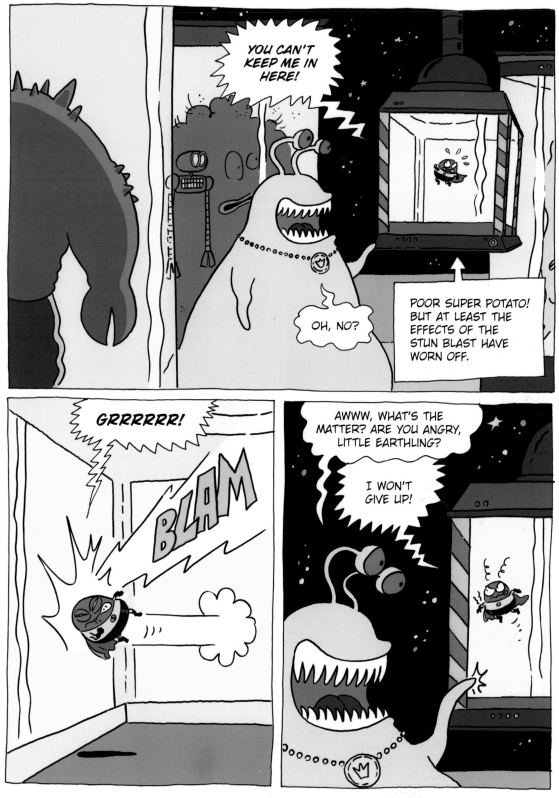

19

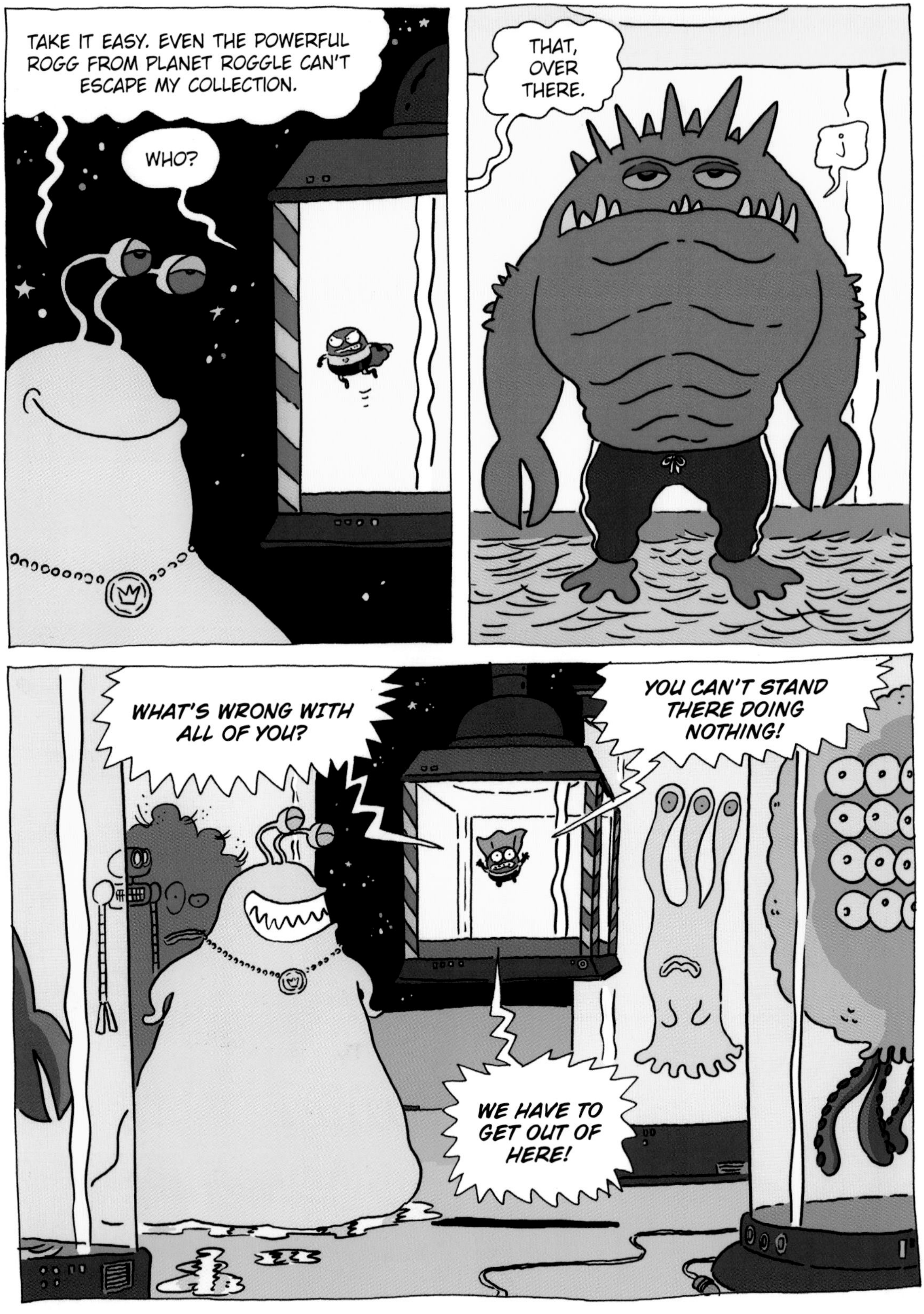
TAKE IT EASY. EVEN THE POWERFUL ROGG FROM PLANET ROGGLE CAN'T ESCAPE MY COLLECTION.
WHO?
THAT, OVER THERE.
¿
WHAT'S WRONG WITH ALL OF YOU?
YOU CAN'T STAND THERE DOING NOTHING!
WE HAVE TO GET OUT OF HERE!

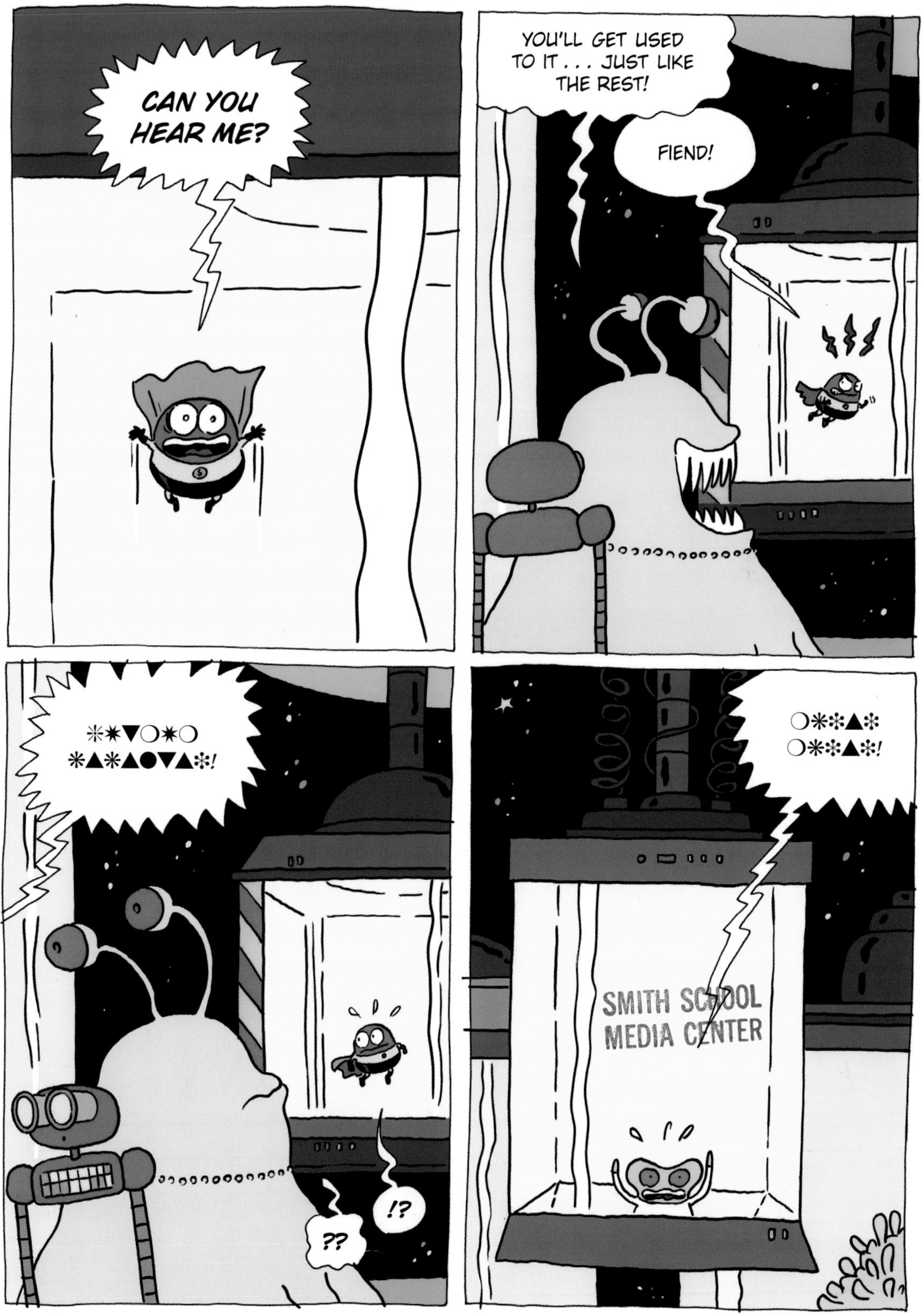
CAN YOU HEAR ME?
YOU'LL GET USED TO IT . . . JUST LIKE THE REST!
FIEND!
??
!?
SMITH SCHOOL MEDIA CENTER

22

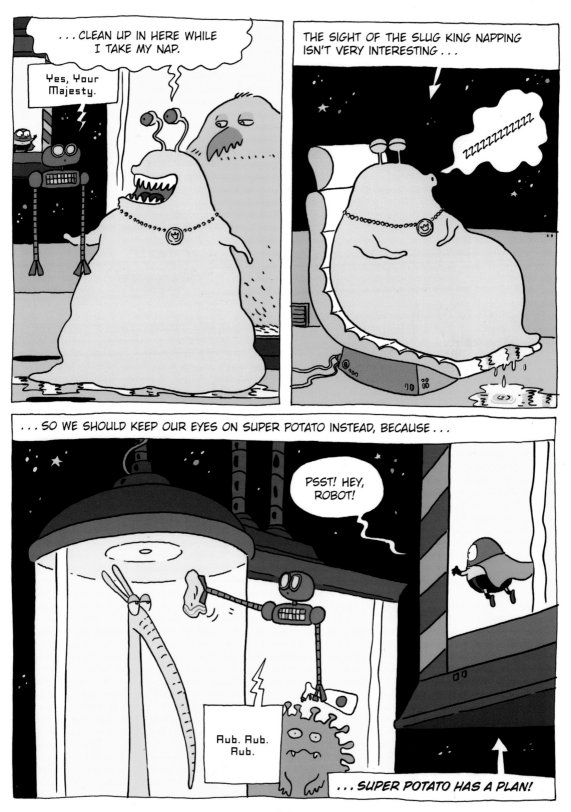

... CLEAN UP IN HERE WHILE I TAKE MY NAP.

Yes, Your Majesty.

THE SIGHT OF THE SLUG KING NAPPING ISN'T VERY INTERESTING . . .

ZZZZZZZZZZZZ

... SO WE SHOULD KEEP OUR EYES ON SUPER POTATO INSTEAD, BECAUSE . . .

PSST! HEY, ROBOT!

Rub. Rub. Rub.

... SUPER POTATO HAS A PLAN!

24

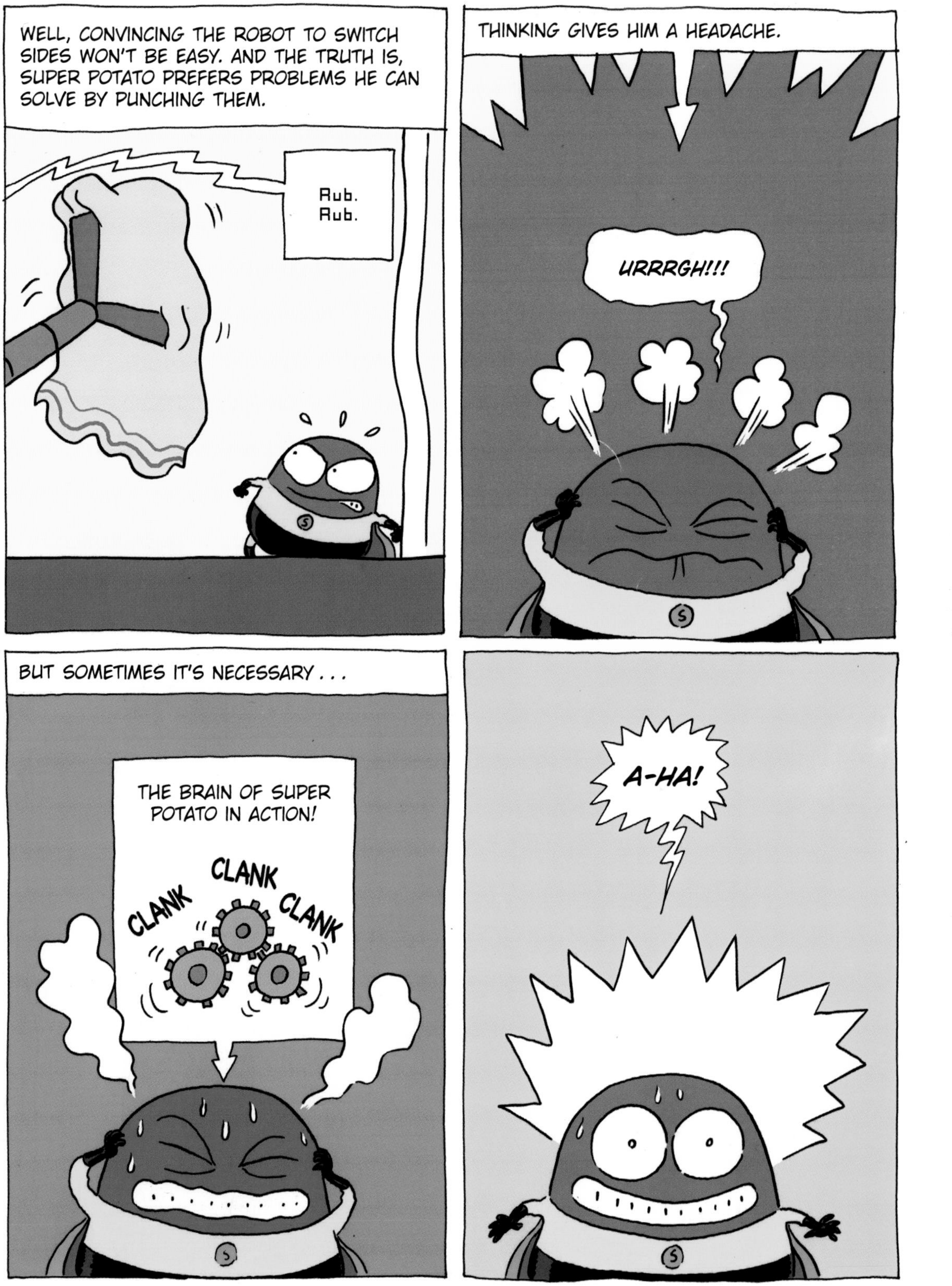
WELL, CONVINCING THE ROBOT TO SWITCH SIDES WON'T BE EASY. AND THE TRUTH IS, SUPER POTATO PREFERS PROBLEMS HE CAN SOLVE BY PUNCHING THEM.
Rub. Rub.
THINKING GIVES HIM A HEADACHE.
URRRGH!!!
BUT SOMETIMES IT'S NECESSARY . . .
THE BRAIN OF SUPER POTATO IN ACTION!
CLANK
CLANK
CLANK
A-HA!

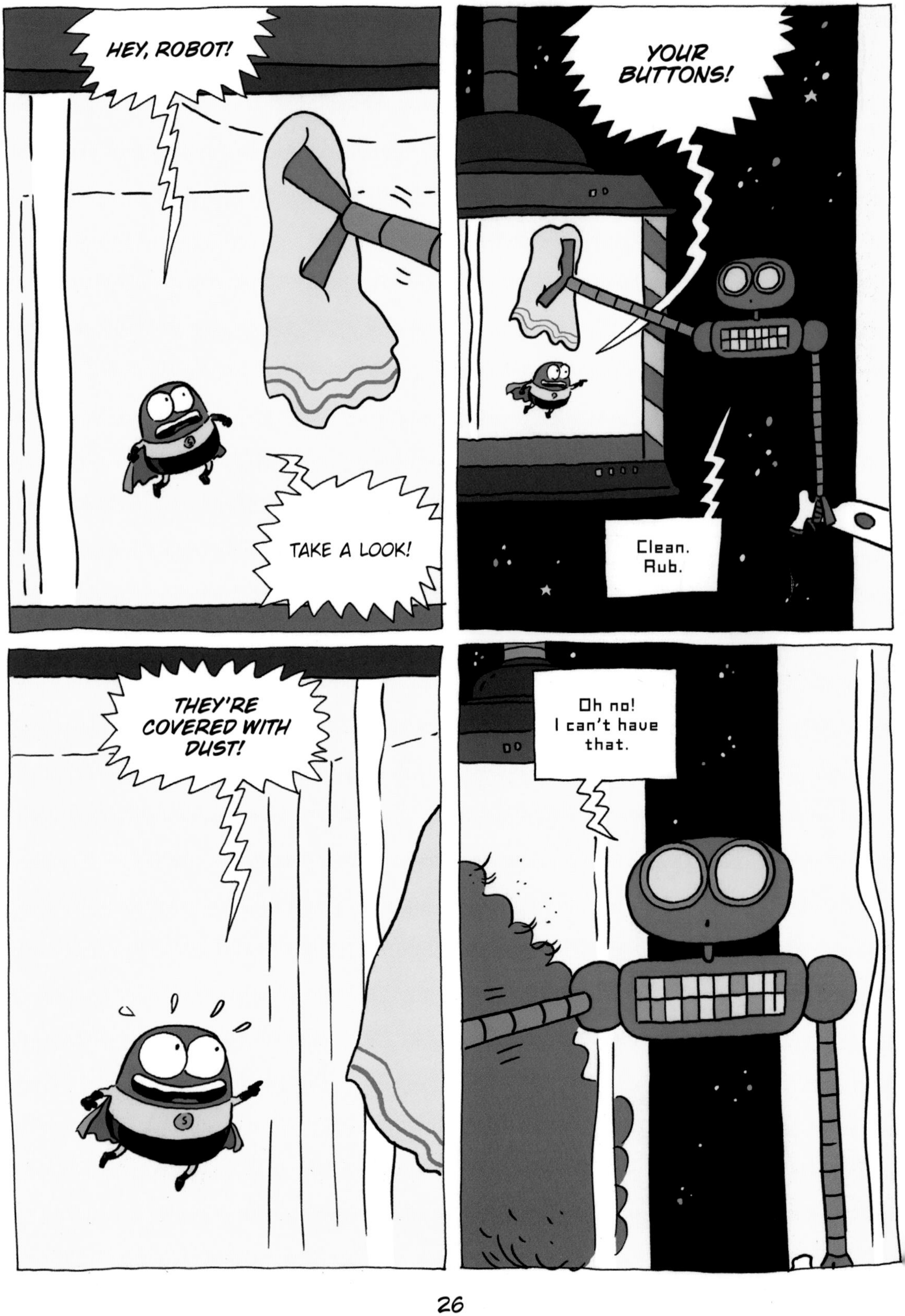
HEY, ROBOT!
YOUR BUTTONS!
TAKE A LOOK!
Clean. Rub.
THEY'RE COVERED WITH DUST!
Oh no! I can't have that.

27

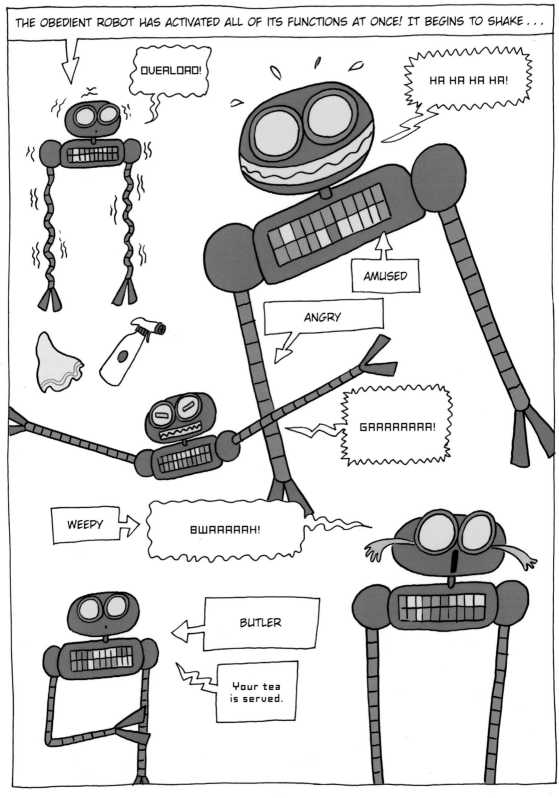

29

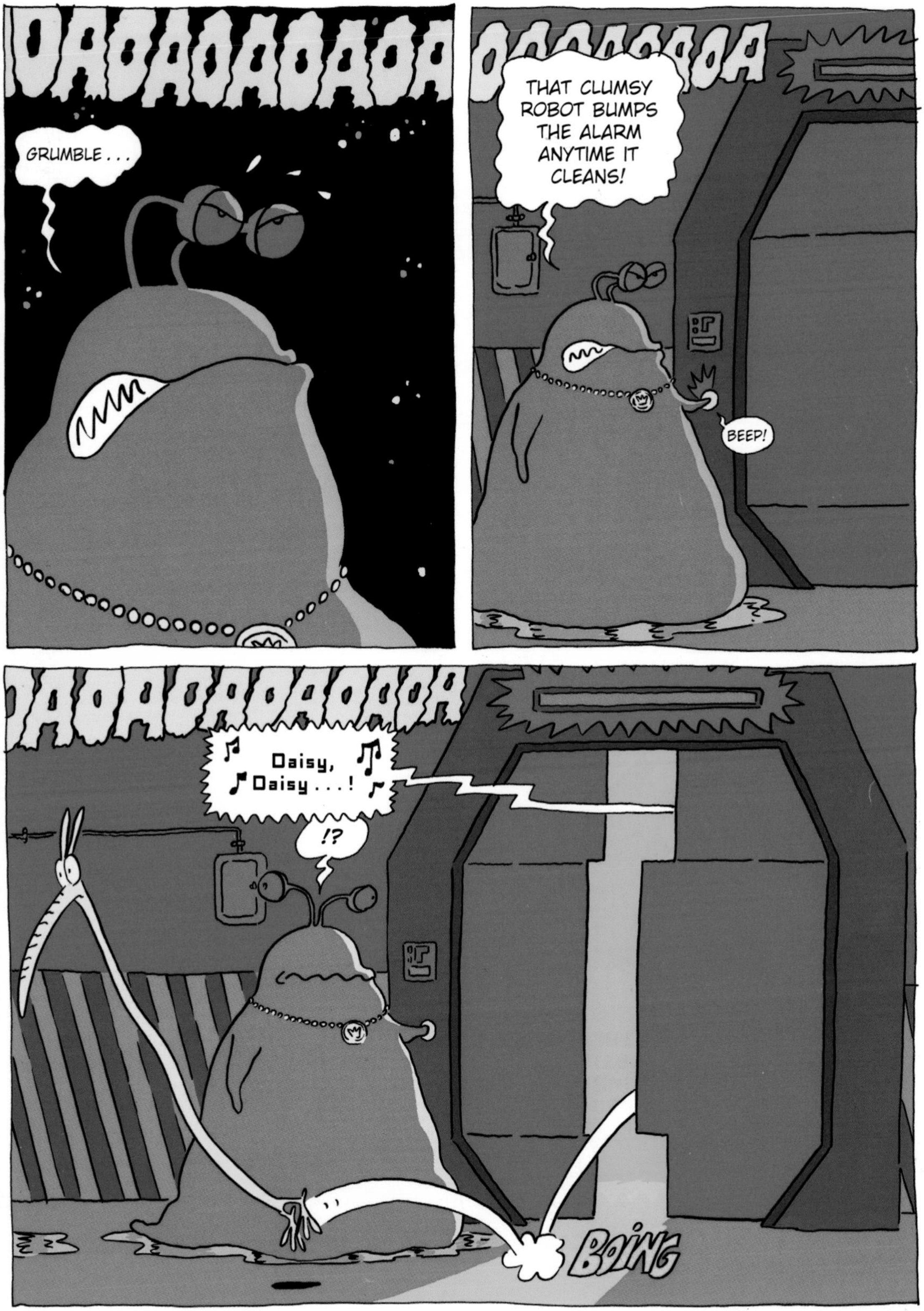

OAOAOAOAOAOAOA
GRUMBLE . . .
OAOAOAOAOA
THAT CLUMSY ROBOT BUMPS THE ALARM ANYTIME IT CLEANS!
BEEP!
OAOAOAOAOAOAOA
Daisy, Daisy . . . !
!?
BOING

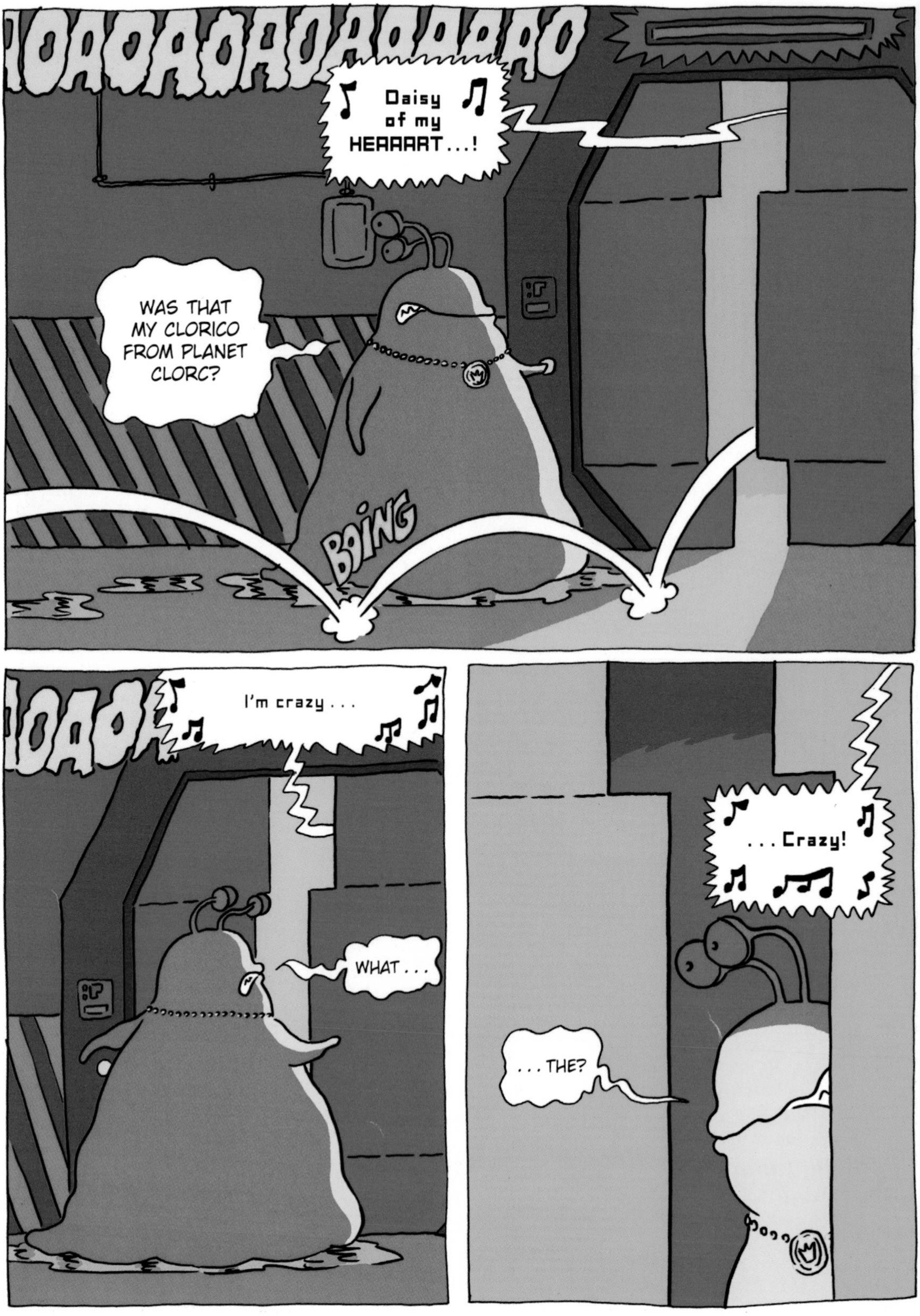
AOAOAOAOAOAOAO
Daisy of my HEAAAAT...!
WAS THAT MY CLORICO FROM PLANET CLORC?
BOING
I'm crazy . . .
WHAT . . .
. . . Crazy!
. . . THE?

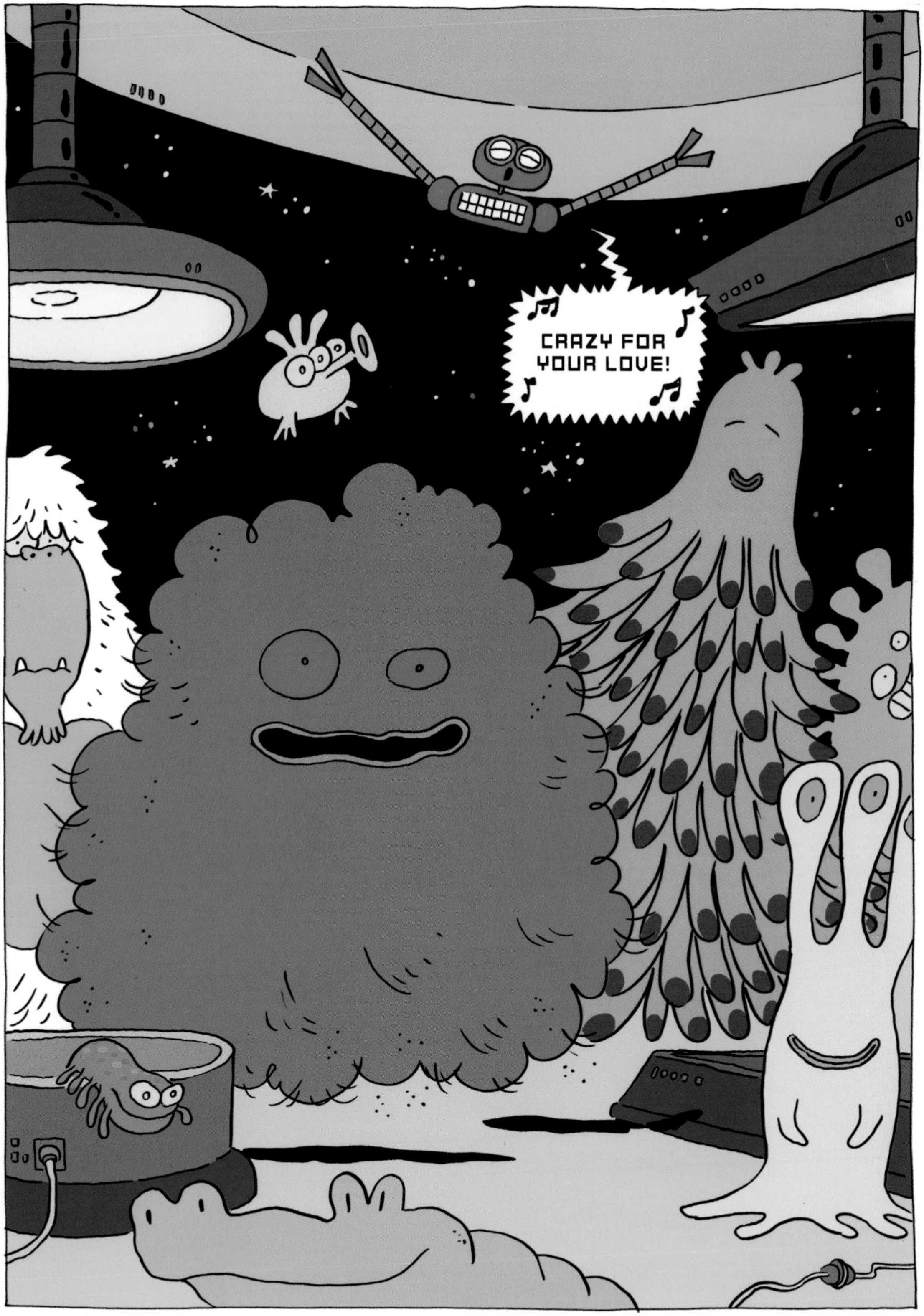
CRAZY FOR YOUR LOVE!

36

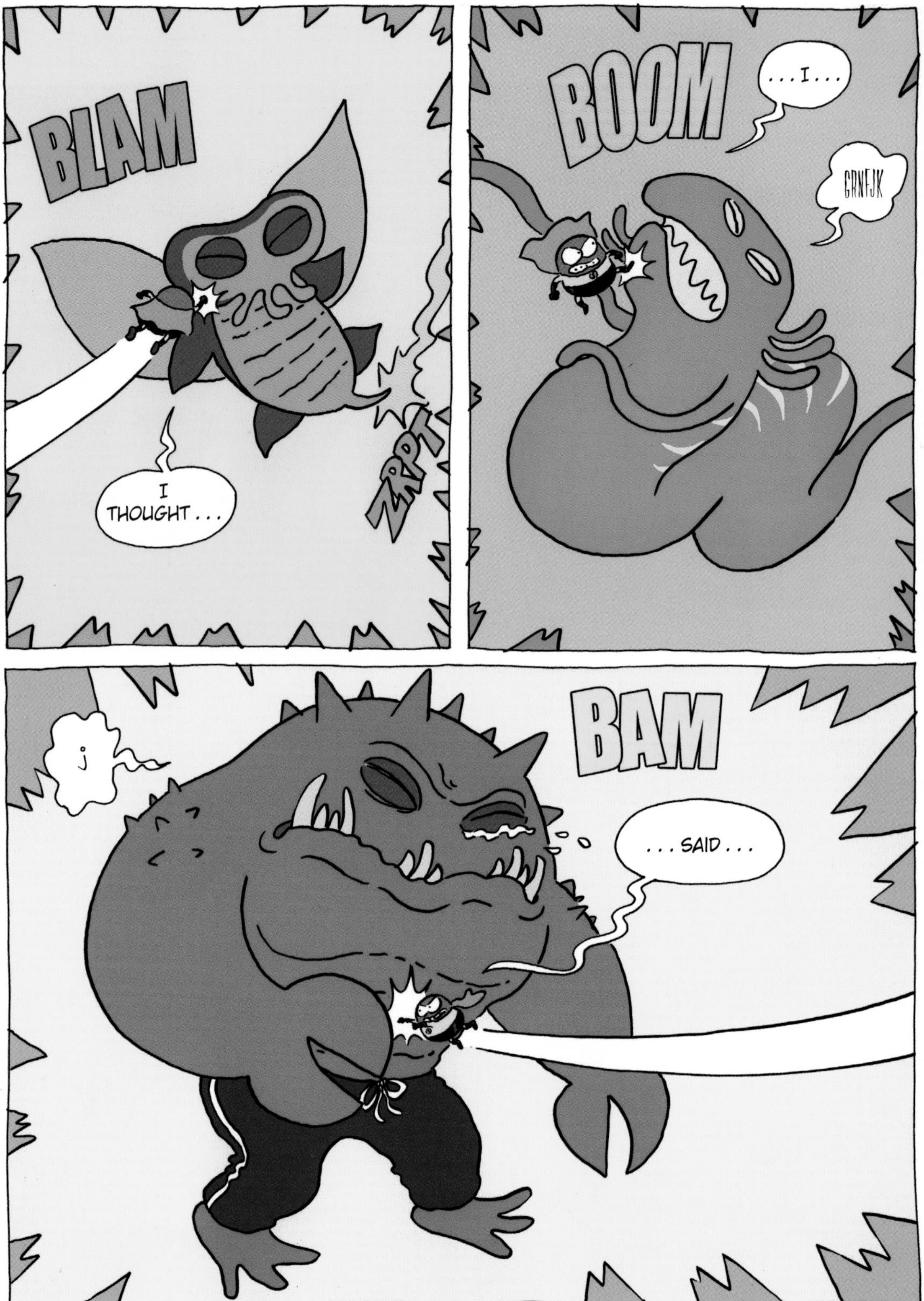
BLAM
I THOUGHT . . .
ZRPT
BOOM
. . . I . . .
GRNFJK
BAM
j
. . . SAID . . .

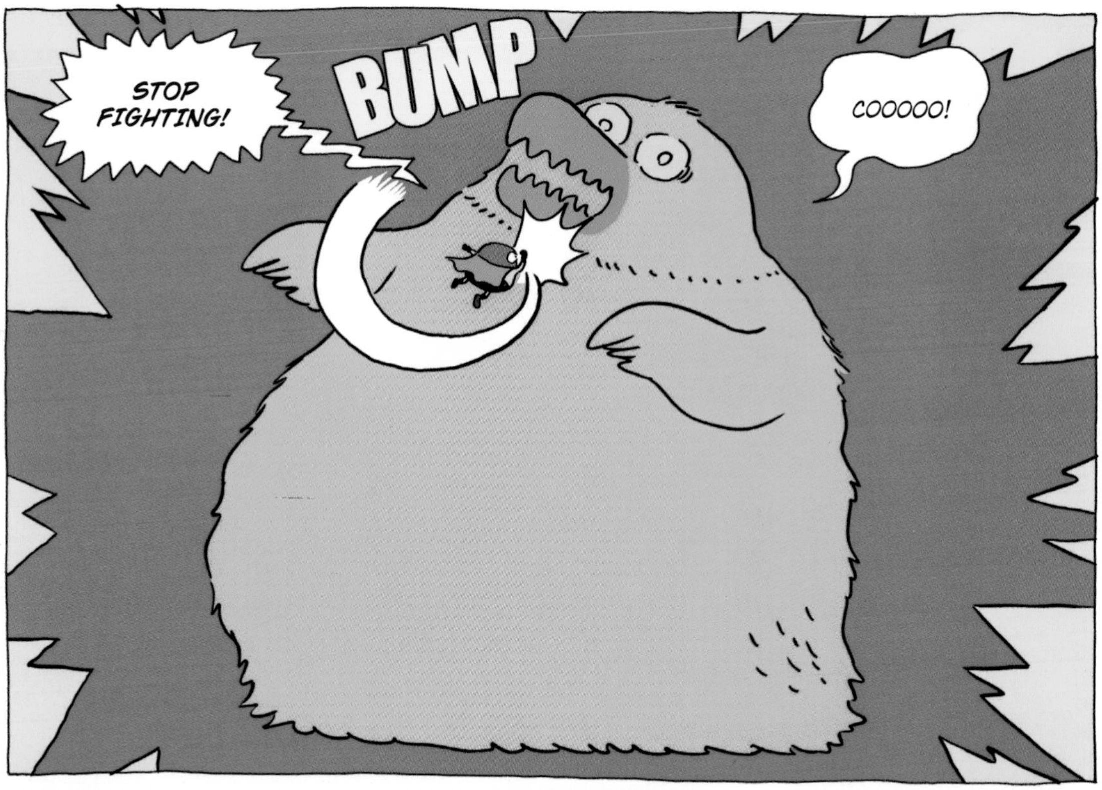
STOP FIGHTING!
BUMP
COOOOO!

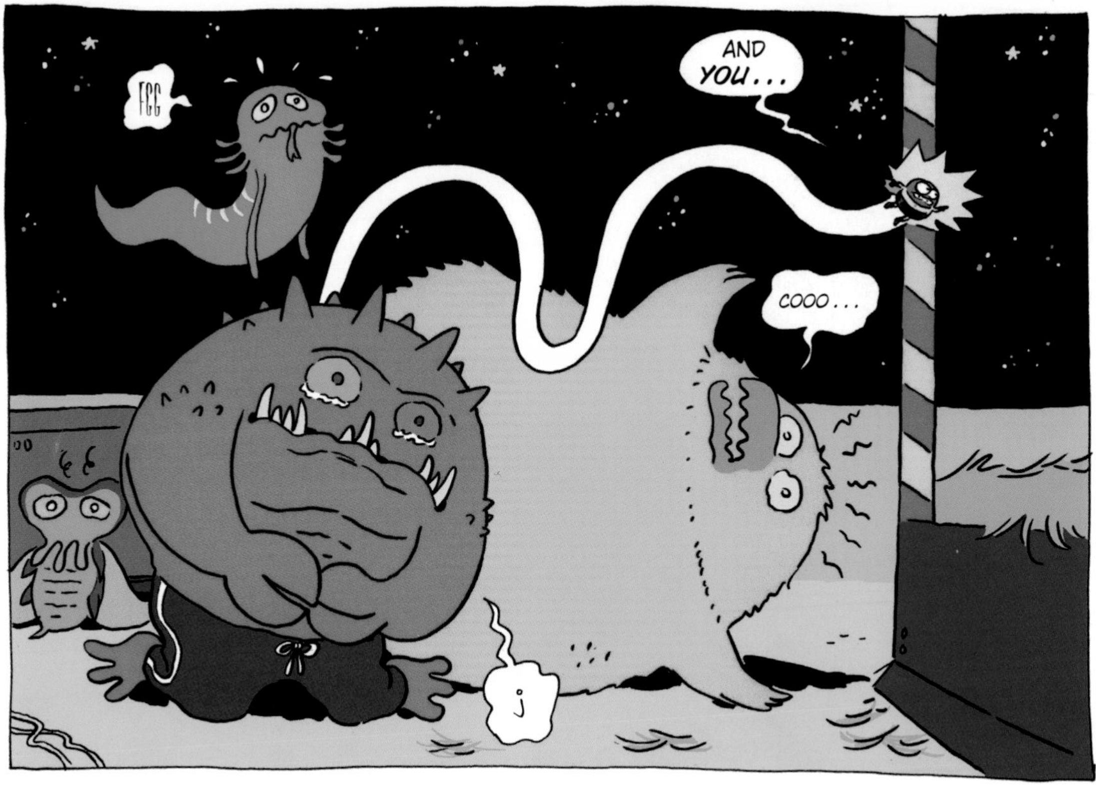
FGG
AND YOU...
COOO...
j

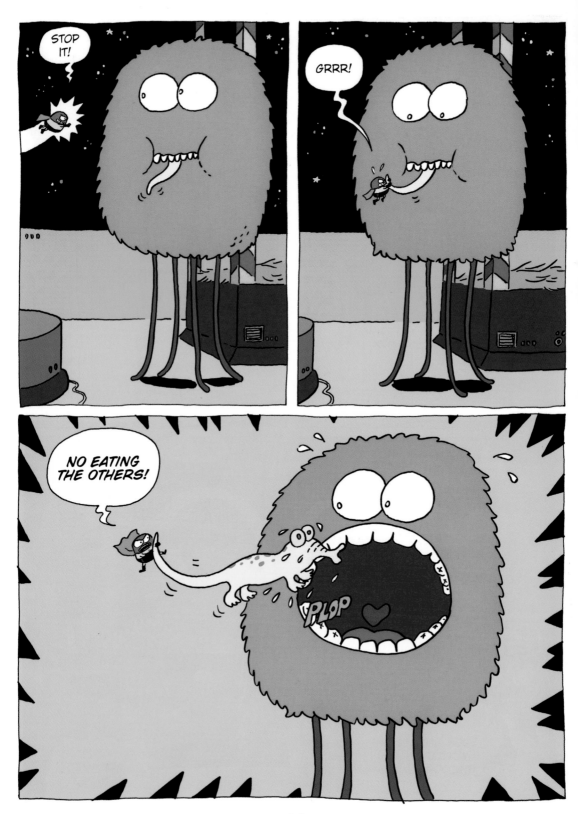

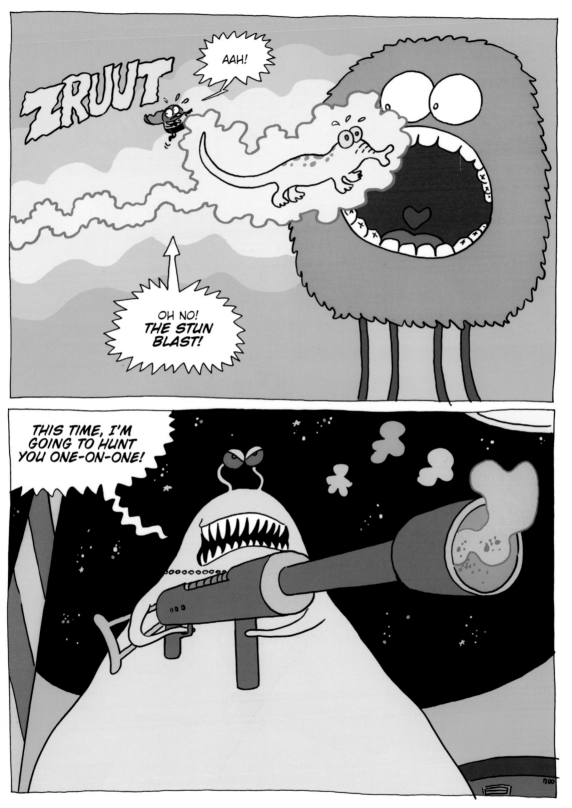

43

46

47

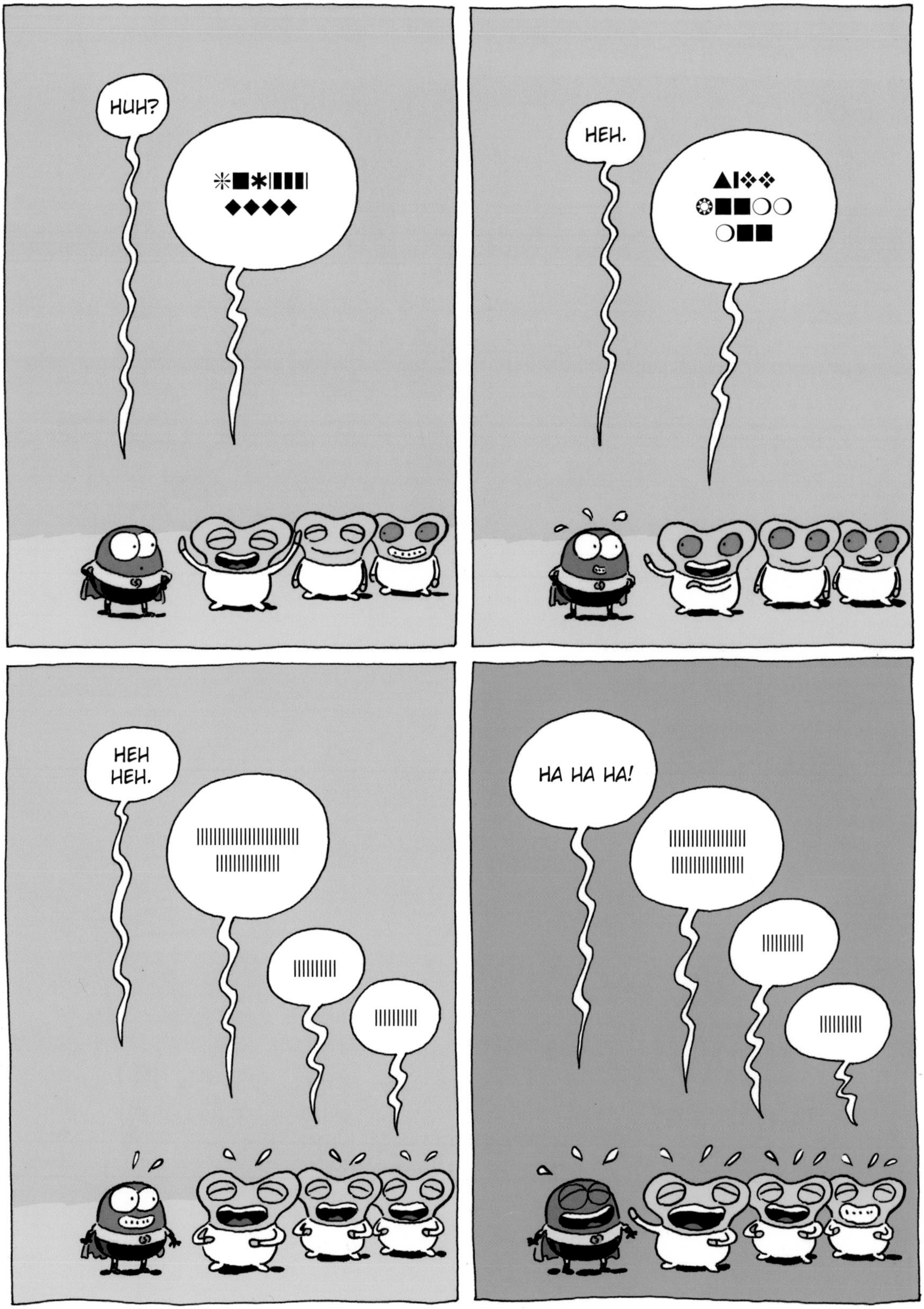
HUH?
HEH.
HEH HEH.
HA HA HA!

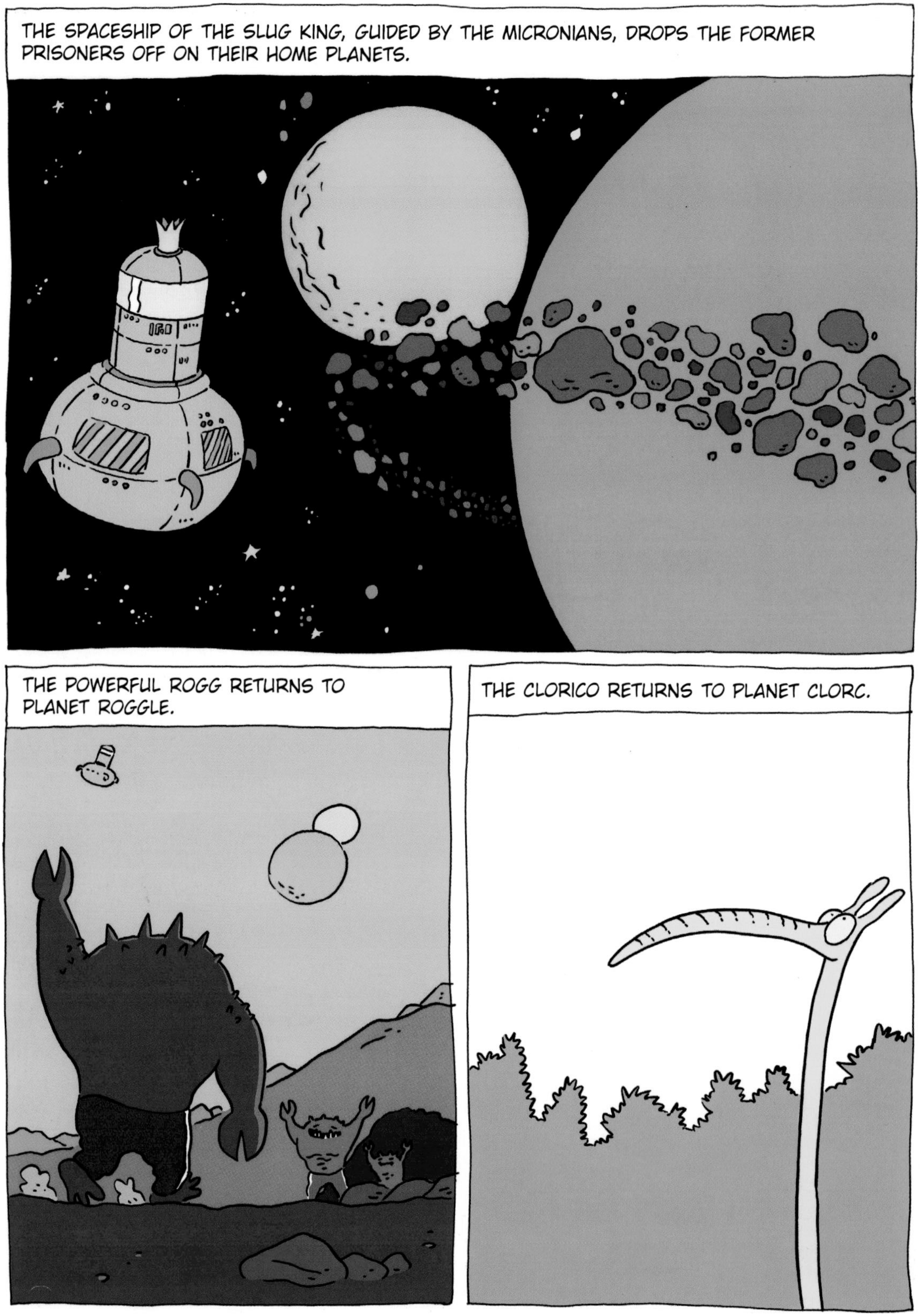
THE SPACESHIP OF THE SLUG KING, GUIDED BY THE MICRONIANS, DROPS THE FORMER PRISONERS OFF ON THEIR HOME PLANETS.
THE POWERFUL ROGG RETURNS TO PLANET ROGGLE.
THE CLORICO RETURNS TO PLANET CLORC.

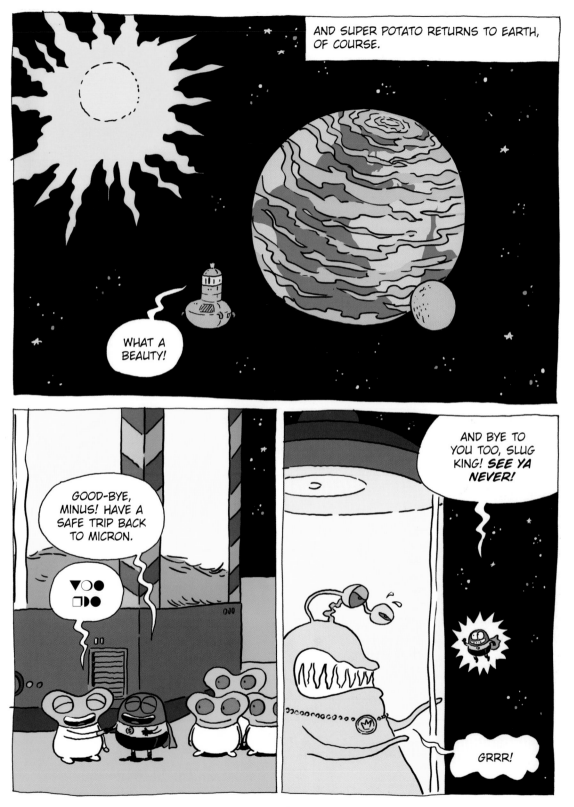

AND SUPER POTATO RETURNS TO EARTH, OF COURSE.

WHAT A BEAUTY!

GOOD-BYE, MINUS! HAVE A SAFE TRIP BACK TO MICRON.

▼○●
□▷●

AND BYE TO YOU TOO, SLUG KING! *SEE YA NEVER!*

GRRR!

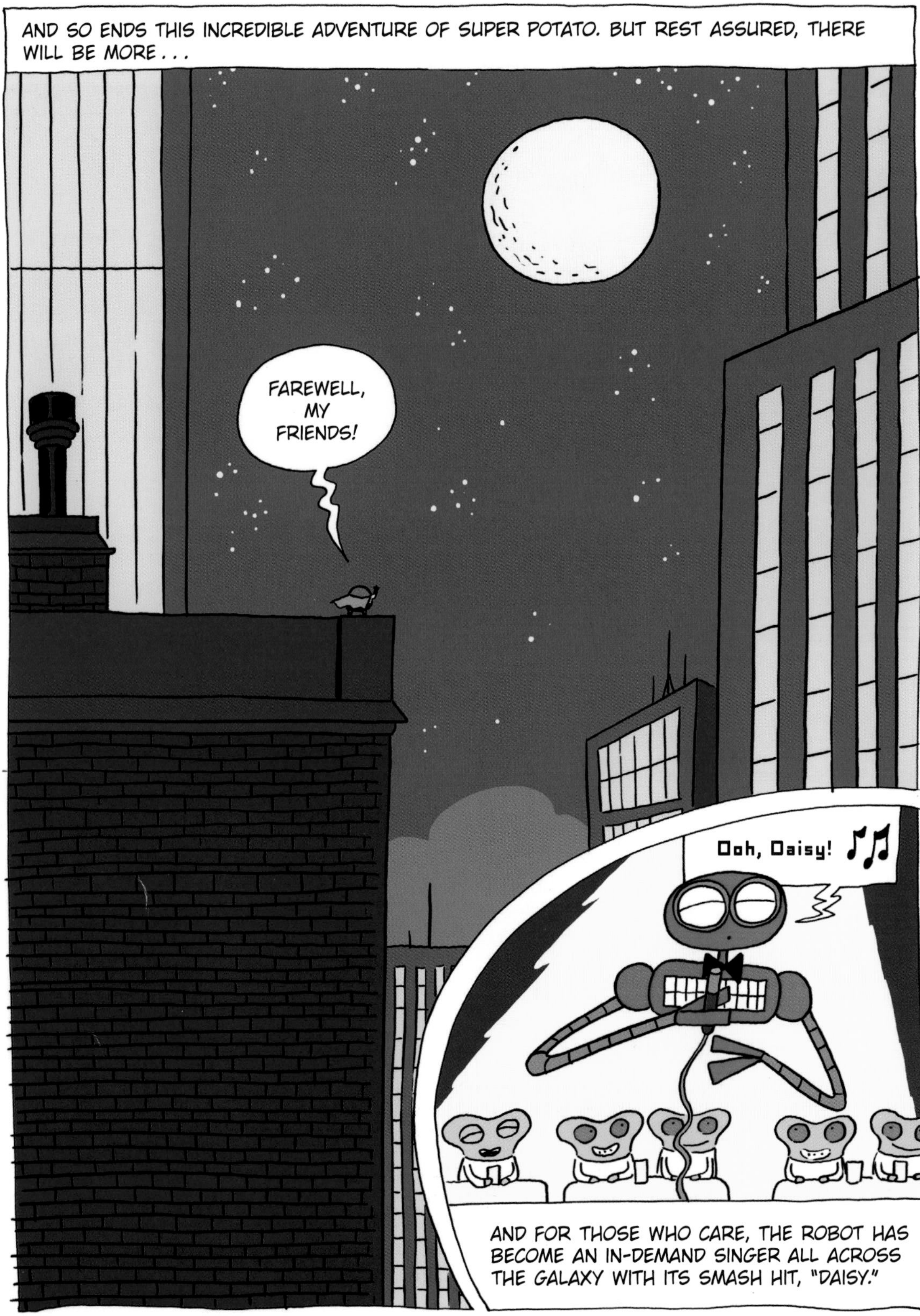
AND SO ENDS THIS INCREDIBLE ADVENTURE OF SUPER POTATO. BUT REST ASSURED, THERE WILL BE MORE . . .
FAREWELL, MY FRIENDS!
Ooh, Daisy!
AND FOR THOSE WHO CARE, THE ROBOT HAS BECOME AN IN-DEMAND SINGER ALL ACROSS THE GALAXY WITH ITS SMASH HIT, "DAISY."

SUPER POTATO

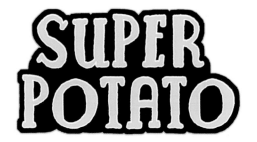

Also available:
The first adventure in the Super Potato saga,

THE EPIC ORIGIN OF SUPER POTATO

SUPER POTATO
#1 THE EPIC ORIGIN OF SUPER POTATO

FROM HERO TO POTATO . . . TO HERO AGAIN!

Super Max has it all. He's a superhero with a flashy uniform and a great head of hair. Sure, sometimes the evil Dr. Malevolent pops up to cause trouble. But Super Max has defeated the villain over and over again.

This time is different. This time, Dr. Malevolent's plan works . . . and he turns the handsome hero into a tiny tuber! But there's one thing the doctor didn't count on. The potato still has powers, and justice takes many forms. Super Max may be gone . . . but it's Super Potato's time to fly!

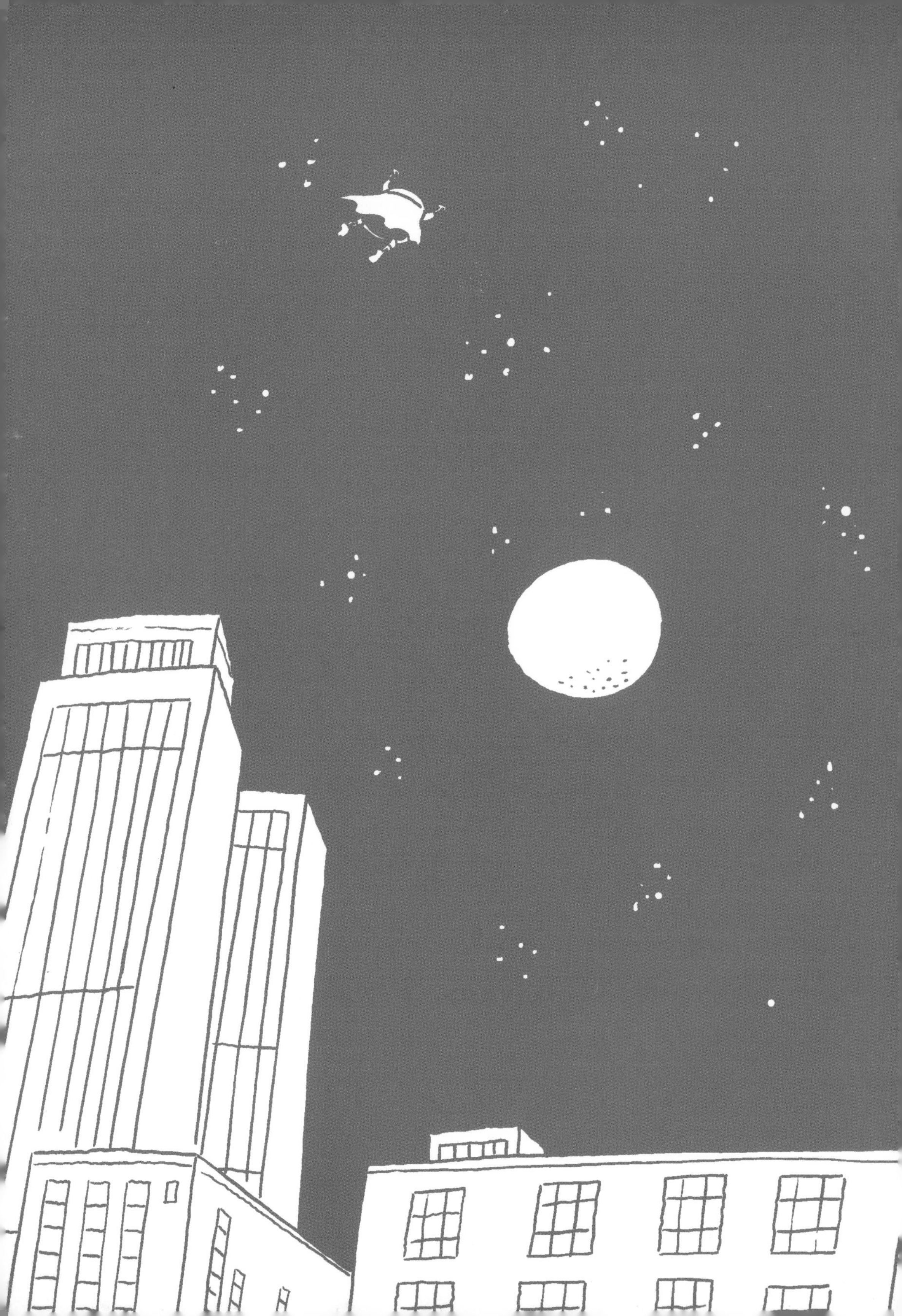